THE CASE OF THE
ONE-EYED KILLER STUD HORSE

· John R. Erickson ·

Illustrations by Gerald L. Holmes

Maverick Books
Published by Gulf Publishing Company
Houston, Texas

This book is dedicated to all the farm and ranch wives who have to put up with noisy kids, ornery husbands, and sorry dogs.

10 9 8 7 6 5

Maverick Books
Published by Gulf Publishing Company
P.O. Box 2608 Houston, Texas 77252-2608

Hank the Cowdog is a registered trademark of John R. Erickson.

Book and cover design by Tom Hair.

Library of Congress Cataloging-in-Publication Data

Erickson, John R., 1943–
     The case of the one-eyed killer stud horse / John R. Erickson: illustrations by Gerald L. Holmes.
          p.   cm.
     At head of title: Hank the Cowdog.
     "The eighth exciting adventure in the Hank the Cowdog series".
     Summary: Hank the cowdog goes to the rescue as a wild, one-eyed horse creates havoc on the ranch but some of his outrageous stunts get him into more trouble than he bargained for.
     ISBN 0-87719-144-1 (pbk.).—ISBN 0-87719-145-X (hbk.).—ISBN 0-87719-146-8 (cassette)
     1. Dogs—Fiction. [1. Dogs—Fiction. 2. Mystery and detective stories. 3. Humorous stories. 4. West (U.S.)—Fiction.] I. Holmes, Gerald L., ill. II. Title.
PS3555.R428H287   1990
813'.54—dc20
[Fic]   90-13571
                                                              CIP
Printed in the United States of America.   AC

Contents

Have you read all of Hank's adventures?
Available in paperback at $6.95:

All books are available on audio cassette too!
($15.95 for two cassettes)

Also available on cassettes:
Hank the Cowdog's Greatest Hits!

CHAPTER

1

THE CASE OF THE CODED TRANSMISSION

It's me again, Hank the Cowdog. Fall is a beautiful time of the year in the Texas Panhandle, or so I thought before the relatives descended upon the ranch for the Thanksgiving holidays and Sally May went lame in her right leg and I found myself involved in the Case of the One-eyed Killer Stud Horse.

Sounds pretty exciting, huh? Just wait until you meet Tuerto, the One-eyed Killer Stud Horse. He'll scare the children so bad, they'll have to sleep with their mothers and dads for a whole week. They'll see his gotch eye in their dreams, and if they're not careful, they're liable to wet the bed.

Any of you kids who wet the bed, don't mention my name. Don't mention *your* name either. Just pretend it didn't happen. When Mom and Dad wake up in the night and find that big cold wet spot in the middle of the bed, tell 'em that it rained during the night and the roof leaked.

Where was I? Under the gas tanks, one of my favorite spots on the ranch and the place where many of my adventures seem to begin. Drover and I were asleep on our gunny sack beds, having returned at daylight from our patrols around the ranch.

Little did we know what adventures lay in store for us because we were catching a few winks of sleep after putting in a long night of patrol work. I've already said that, but it doesn't hurt to repeat yourself repeat yourself once in a while in a while.

I love to sleep. Sometimes I dream about bones and long juicy strips of steak fat. I remember one dream in particular when Sally May drove up to the gas tanks and unloaded a strip of steak fat that was half a mile long. That was a dream to remember. It took me two weeks to eat that strip of steak fat. When I was done, I couldn't walk. Had to crawl around on all-fours with a roller skate under my belly.

That was one of my all-time great dreams. Another involved a fifty foot steak bone, I

2

mean a bone as big as a tree. Took me a month and a half to eat that rascal. After I'd finished, I was telling Drover about how I'd just by George destroyed a steak bone that looked like a tree.

He gave me his usual stupid expression and said, "You mean you ate that tree that looked like a steak bone?"

I didn't pay any attention to him, but I spent the next three months sneezing sawdust, which made me wonder. That was all in a dream, of course.

Bone-dreams and steakfat-dreams are wonderful, but perhaps the wonderfulest dreams of all are the ones that star Beulah the Collie.

Ah, Sweet Beulah! Be still my heart! Return to thy cage of ribs and venture not forth into the dark night of darkness like a stalking jungle beast venturing and stalking through the inky dark blackness of . . . something. Love, I guess.

Mercy. Just the thought of that woman gets me in an uproar. Just mention her name and suddenly the same mouth that reduces trees to sawdust and pulverizes monsters begins gushing poetry. Beats anything I ever saw.

Experts will tell you that I'm a very lucky dog. I mean, it ain't every dog that has the honor of falling in love with the most beautiful collie gal in the whole entire world. Even more experts would tell you how lucky SHE is.

Boy, is she lucky, but sometimes I wonder if she knows it. She keeps showing up with that birddog. I just don't understand . . . oh well. In my dreams she belongs to me. I don't allow birddogs into my dreams.

Anyways, me and Drover were under the gas tanks, melted and molded into our gunny sacks, and throwing up long lines of Z's, when all of a sudden I heard Drover say, "Zebras wear pajamas but you can't spot a leopard with a spyglass."

Without opening my eyes or bringing myself to the Full Alert Mode, I ran that statement through my data banks. All at once, it didn't make sense, so I lifted one ear to intercept any other transmissions, shall we say, from my pipsqueak assistant. Sure enough, I picked up another.

"There's no pullybones in a chicken sandwich."

This one made me suspicious, so I opened one eye. Drover appeared to be 100% asleep, yet he continued to transmit messages in a code I had never run across before. I listened.

"If you take the dog out of doggerel, the

4

motor won't start without peanut butter."

Ah ha! A certain pattern began to emerge. I opened both eyes, cranked myself up to a sitting position, and listened more carefully. What I had originally taken to be the incoherent ramblings of Drover's so-called mind were showing signs of being something else—perhaps coded messages from some magic source?

How else could you explain Drover's use of a big word like "doggerel?" Or his reference to zebras and leopards and auto mechanics? I knew for a fact that Drover had never seen a zebra or a leopard, and I had reason to suspect that he didn't know peanuts about starting motors.

Your ordinary dog would have dismissed it all as nonsense and gone back to sleep, but as you might have already surmised, I decided to probe this thing a little deeper. I moved closer and listened. He spoke again.

"When the sun rises in the morning in the east, the biscuits rise in the oven in the yeast."

Hmm, yes. This message not only rhymed, but it also hinted at some deep, profoundical meaning. This transmission had to be originating from some mysterious source outside of Drover.

5

I decided to draw him out with a clever line of questions. It was risky. I mean, the sound of my voice might very well wake him up and spoil everything, but that was a risk I had to take.

What we had here was The Case of the Coded Transmission, and at last the clues were beginning to fall into place. Your ordinary dogs, your poodles and your cheewahwahs and your cocker spaniels, would miss all of the important stuff. I mean, it would go right over their heads like a duck out of water.

So there I was, sifting clues and finding patterns and preparing clever questions that would draw even more startling revelations from the mind of my sleeping assistant. As I said, it was a risky procedure but I had to give it a try.

"All right, Drover. You hear my voice, is that correct?"

"Mumbo jumbo."

"Does that mean 'yes' in your secret code?"

"Jumbo mumbo."

"Are you trying to reverse the code on me now?"

"Mumbo hocus pocus."

"What happened to jumbo?"

"Jumbo hocus pocus."

"Thought you could fool me, didn't you? You should have known better. As I've often said, Drover, it isn't the size of the dog in the fight that matters. It's the size of the fog in the dog."

"Foggy doggy mumbo jumbo."

"Exactly. I've locked into your code now. You can hear my voice, Drover, and you

G.L.Holmes

will do exactly as I say. You will answer my questions . . .''

"Gargle murgle guttersnipe."

". . . but not until I ask them. Stand by for the first question. Ready? Mark! Here is the first question: Give me the full name of the mysterious source of these messages.''

"Mumble grumble mutter."

"You're muttering, Drover, I can't understand what you're saying.''

"Mumble grumble rumble."

"That's better. Is that the full name of the mysterious source of these messages?''

"Murgle gurgle snore zzzzzzzz.''

"Hmmm. Obviously he's not from around here. That's a foreign name if I ever heard one. Any name with that many Z's in it is bound to be foreign.''

"Chicken feather jelly."

"What? Repeat that message and concentrate on your diction.''

"Dictionary jelly murgle snore."

"That's better. All right, Drover, this brings us to our last and most important question, to the darkness behind the veil, so to speak. What is the evil purpose behind these coded messages sent to you from the mysterious foreign source?''

8

I held my breath and waited. Suddenly, the screen door slammed up at the house. Drover leaped to his feet. His eyes popped open, revealing . . .

Very little, actually. His ears were crooked, his eyes were crossed. He staggered two steps to the left and two steps to the right.

"Scraps!" he said in a squeaky voice.

"What? Is that the evil purpose of all these messages?"

"What are you talking about?"

"You know exactly what I'm talking about. Answer the question."

"Sally May just came out of the house. I bet she's got some scraps from breakfast."

G. L. Holmes

"Huh?" At last it all fit together. "You're exactly right, Drover. And speaking of evil purposes, unless we do some fancy stepping, the cat will beat us to the scraps. Come on, Drover, to the yard gate!"

And so it was that, having solved The Case of the Coded Transmission, we turned to more serious business—delivering Pete the Barncat his first defeat of the day.

CHAPTER

2

STRICKEN WITH SNEEZAROMA BECAUSE SHE WHACKED ME ON THE NOSE WITH A WOODEN SPOON

We went streaking up the hill, with me in the lead and Drover bringing up the rear. When we got to the yard gate, I glanced around and saw that we had succeeded in our first objective.

Sally May and Loper were there talking, but Pete was nowhere in sight. Ha ha, ho ho! In her right hand, Sally May held a plate, in her left a wooden spoon.

I turned to my assistant and gave him a worldly smile. "This is going to be a piece of cake, Drover."

11

"Oh boy! Usually it's burned toast and a busted egg."

"What?"

"I said, usually it's burned toast . . ."

"I heard that, Drover, but it shows that you misunderstood what I said."

"Oh."

" 'Piece of cake' is an expression, a figure of speech. It means, 'This is going to be easy.' "

"Oh. Well, that's easy enough."

"Exactly. You see, Drover, sometimes our words have subtle meanings that go beyond the actual words. That's the beauty of language, its many shades of meaning."

"Yeah, and on a hot day that shade sure comes in handy."

"Exactly. So there you are, son, a little lesson in the endless variety of language."

"It's pretty good, all right. Sure hope it's chocolate."

"What?"

"I've never had chocolate cake in the morning."

For a moment I considered giving the runt a tongue lashing, but just then Loper spoke up.

"Hon, I'm going over to check that fence between us and Billy's west pasture. His stud horse got through the fence yesterday and I found him in the home pasture. I don't want that crazy thing coming up around the house. He could hurt someone."

"Oh my!"

"He's got a mean streak and only one eye. I wouldn't want to take any chances with you or Little Alfred. He's kind of dangerous."

Loper turned his eyes on me. I gave him a big smile and wagged my tail and went over and jumped up on him. Licked him on the hand too. I wanted to build up a few Loyal Dog Points, see. In this line of work, a guy needs to get points in the bank any time he can.

Anyways, I jumped up on Loper, said howdy, wished him good morning, and, you know, let him know that I was there on the job. He looked down into my face, curled his lip, and pushed me away.

"Get down! You stink."

HUH? Well, I . . .

"If we had a dog on this ranch that was worth anything," he wiped his hand on his jeans, "we wouldn't have to worry about Billy's stud horse. Anyway, when the cousins get here, don't let them play in the pasture."

"All right. They'll be here around eleven. Will you be home for lunch?"

"I don't know. I've got to help the neighbors move some cattle around. I might be late getting home."

While they were talking, Sally May held the plate about waist-high. I got kind of curious as to what tasty morsels might be on it, so I hopped up on my back legs and took a peek.

Hmmm. Scrambled eggs, five or six fatty ends of bacon, and two pieces of burned toast. Burned toast must have been one of Sally May's specialties, because she seemed to crank out two or three pieces of it every morning.

I'm not too crazy about burned toast, but fatty ends of bacon . . . I can get worked up over fatty ends of bacon.

Sally May had got herself caught up in a conversation and had forgotten to scrape our goodies out on the ground, is what had happened, and it suddenly occurred to me that that plate was probably getting pretty heavy.

I mean, you don't think about fatty ends of bacon weighing very much, but you take enough of them and put them together and you'll come up with a whole entire hog that might weigh, oh, three-four hundred pounds. (That's where bacon comes from, don't you know. Hogs. Big hogs.)

Now, Sally May was a tough old gal but she

14

had her limits. I'd seen her bucking bales of alfalfa on the hay wagon and I'd seen her carrying sacks of chicken feed from her car into the machine shed, but I'd never seen her lift a three hundred pound hog. Even Loper couldn't do that.

She had no business lifting hogs. I mean, here was the mother of a small child. Didn't she have enough to do, keeping up the house and the garden and the chickens, caring for a child and a husband? Seemed to me it was my duty to lighten her load a little bit.

I've always figgered that one of the reasons we're put here on this earth is to help others. That's why, when I have a chance to ease someone else's burden, I try to do it.

And let me tell you, it wasn't an easy thing to do. I mean, there I was standing on my back legs, and I had to turn my head to the side, ease my nose over the edge of the plate, and snag the bacon ends with my tongue.

You ever try to snag something with your tongue, when your head's turned sideways? It sounds easy, but you can take my word for it, it ain't. I'm not sure why. A guy's tongue ought to work just as well sideways as up and down. I mean, why should a tongue care which way is up and which is down?

Beats me, but the point is that it was a difficult maneuver. No ordinary dog would have even attempted it. I not only attempted it but came *that close* to pulling it off. Here's how I did it. (You might want to jot down a few notes.)

First, I extended my tongue to its fully-extended position, at which point I had something like six inches of powerful tongue reeled out of my mouth. Second, I concentrated all my powers of concentration on putting a curl into the end of it.

Pretty tough.

Thirdly, with the same curl in the end of the same tongue we have been discussing, I began easing a bacon end over toward the edge of the plate, even though the root of my tongue was getting tired from the strain of being fully extended. (Try it and see if the root of your tongue doesn't get tired.)

Fourthly, just as I was about to throw a coil of tongue around the juicy end of bacon fat, reel it back into my mouth, and gobble it down, Sally May saw what I was doing and smacked me on the nose with the wooden spoon.

"Get down, Hank! I'll feed you when Pete gets here."

In other words, she had misinterpreted my intentions. Maybe she thought I was merely trying to steal the bacon before her stupid and greedy cat arrived to hog it all. Not a bad idea, actually, but of course I had higher motives.

On this outfit, it seems to be all right for a cat to be a hog, but let a dog try to be a hog just once and WHACK! He gets it across the nose with a wooden spoon.

It ain't fair, but let's don't get started on that.

I turned to Drover. "What are you grinning about?"

"Who me?"

"I saw that silly grin on your face. I'd advise you to wipe it off before . . ."

That whack on the nose had a strange effect on me, made me sneeze. I'm not talking about one little sneeze or even two, I'm talking about a bunch of BIG ones, all in a row, one after another, bang-bang-bang—or sneeze-sneeze-sneeze, you might say. And each one of them sneezes just about blew the end of my nose off.

This is a fairly rare medical condition known as "Sneezaroma." Those who get it never forget it, because you can't stop sneezing.

Drover still had that silly grin on his face.

"Bless you."

"Thank you."

"You're welcome. You got hay fever?"

"No, I don't have ACHOOOO! Hay fever."

"Bless you."

"Thank you."

"You're welcome. Sure sounds like hay fever to me."

"Sounds can be deceiving, son. Just because I sneeze, that doesn't mean I have ACHOOOO!"

"Bless you. I have hay fever too, so I know how it feels."

"I just told you, Numbskull, I *don't have hay fever.* Sally May hit me on the nose with a spoon and it gave me Sneezaroma. Let's ACHOO drop it."

"Bless you."

"Thank you."

"You're welcome. Maybe you're allergic to spoons. ACHOO! Gosh, maybe I'm allergic to your sneezes."

"Bless you."

"Thanks, Hank."

"You're welcome. No, I don't think so, Drover. More than likely it's just ACHOO!"

"Bless you."

"Thank you."

18

"You're welcome. ACHOO!"
"Bless you."
"Thanks, Hank."
"You're ACHOO!"
"Bless ACHOO!"

G. L. Holmes

"Thank you, and bless you ACHOO!"

"ACHOOO!"

"ACHOOO!"

We were getting nowhere fast. Carrying on an intelligent conversation with Drover is hard enough under the best of conditions, but when we're both sneezing, it's very near impossible.

I was all set to head back down to the gas tanks and put my poor nose to bed, when all at once I saw something that made the hair stand up on the back of my neck. Prancing down the hill from the machine shed was one of my least favorite characters on the ranch— my arch-enemy, to be exact.

Pete the Barncat.

He had his stupid tail stuck straight up in the air and he was purring like a little motorboat. No doubt he was coming to hog all the breakfast scraps, but it was my job to see that he failed in his mission of greed.

"Hold up, Drover. Unless I'm badly mistaken, we're fixing to get ourselves into some combat. We've got a cat coming in at two o'clock."

"Well, better late than tardy."

"Exactly. Battle stations, Drover, and prepare for some heavy duty barking!"

"AAAA-CHOOOO!"

"That's not barking."

"I'm sorry."

"You're welcome."

"Thanks, Hank."

And with that, we turned our menacing glares on Pete the Barncat.

G. L. Holmes

CHAPTER

3

THE CASE OF THE EMBEZZLED SCRAMBLED EGGS

I've never understood exactly what it is about Pete that gets me so stirred up. Under ordinary circumstances, I keep an iron grip on my emotions, which comes in handy in the security business because emotions have no place in that spear.

Sphere, I probably should say. I don't like Pete, that's the point. He's your typical arrogant, sniveling, scheming, insolent cat. I don't like the way he holds his tail, the way he walks, or the way he rubs up against everything in sight.

I don't like his face. I don't like his whiney voice. I don't like his attitude. I don't like cats, but I wouldn't like Pete even if he wasn't a cat.

When he appeared on the scene, my ears jumped up and a growl began to rumble deep in my throat. It was just by George automatic.

By this time, Loper had left in his pickup, but Sally May was still there with her plate of goodies, which I had every intention of protecting from Pete. Sally May must have heard me growling.

"Hank, stop that! I won't have you bullying the cat."

I twisted my head around and looked up at her with my most sincere expression of sincerity. Bullying the cat! I hadn't even touched the little snot, much less given him the pounding he so richly deserved.

I whimpered and whapped my tail on the ground.

She bent down and brought her face only inches away from the end of my nose. "I know what you're thinking, Hank, but if you start tormenting the cat again, I'm going to whack you over the head with this spoon."

Suddenly I was seized by an impulse to lick her on the nose. I don't know why. It just seemed the appropriate thing to do. My tongue shot out and gave her a big, loving, juicy, peace-making, forgiving, friendly cowdog lick on the nose.

And it was such a big extra special lick that some of it lapped over and got her on the mouth.

My goodness. You'd have thought that she'd been bitten by a water moccasin, the way she drew back and stiffened up.

"Don't do that! I don't like dogs who lick all the time! No, no, no. *Don't lick.*"

And here's the real shocker. She not only wiped her mouth with the back of her hand, but she *spit.* Or is it "spitted?" "Spat?" She spatted, not at anyone in particular but in a way that made you think she'd just gotten a taste of poison.

Really shocked me. I mean, all those years I'd thought she was a proper lady, and then to see her spitting . . . well, it kind of disappointed me, I guess you'd say. I'd expected more from Sally May than spitting.

I turned to Drover and shrugged. "How do you please these people? They don't want you to growl, they don't want you to bark, they don't want you to hamburgerize the cats. After years and years of working up the courage to show a little affection, you give 'em a lick on the face and, whammo, they throw it right back at you."

"Maybe she doesn't like dogs."

"And once you've been rebuked and reject- ed and scorned, you withdraw into the inner recessitudes of your dark self, and something happens to you, Drover. A guy begins to change in little ways. It makes him hard and cold and hard."

"You said 'hard' twice."

"It makes him think about running away and becoming an outlaw, a killer dog who howls in the night and spends his life looking for revenge."

"I spent all day looking for a bone once."

"Exactly. Yes, rejection is a terrible thing, Drover."

"I guess so. Maybe you'd better not lick her in the face any more."

I stared at the runt. "Is that all you can say? Is that all the comfort you can give me in this time of sorrow?"

"Well . . . you might try it and see if it helps."

"A simple answer from a simple mind. I should have known better than to expose the burning embers of my heart to the likes of you."

"Heartburn's pretty bad, but it beats hay fever."

At that moment, I realized that Pete was rubbing against my right front leg and flicking the end of his tail across my chin. Suddenly, I forgot my sorrows and began thinking nasty thoughts.

"Hi, Hankie. Sure is a pretty day, isn't it?"

My lips curled, my eyes flared, and a growl rumbled in my throat. I glanced up at Sally May. Had she been looking the other way, Pete wouldn't have thought the day was so pretty. But she wasn't looking the other way. She was looking at me.

"Don't you dare! Now, you dogs had better learn to get along with the cat. Here, kitty kitty."

Pete gave me one last grin, stepped on my tail, and shot through a hole in the fence. Then, before my very eyes, Sally May scraped MY juicy, fatty bacon ends out on the ground and gave them all to the cat.

Well, hey, that was too much. I barked. I howled. I cried and moaned and protested this injustice. Sally May came over to the fence and gave me a scowl.

"Oh be quiet, Hank. I've got some for you too. Here." She scraped something off the

27

plate. It hit the ground.

I sniffed it. Scrambled eggs and burned toast. I gave her a mournful look and whapped my tail. I mean, scrambled eggs are okay, but I had sort of prepared my taste buds for something in the bacon department.

I put some serious begs on her. No sale. All right, if scrambled eggs was the best we could do . . . I looked down and was stunned to see that the eggs had vanished. I turned to Drover, who was licking his chops.

"Did you eat my eggs?"

"Who me?"

"Of course you did. Yes, it's all coming clear now. First the cat steals my bacon, then my own trusted assistant embezzles my eggs. Oh vile world! Oh wickedness! Oh treachery! How much deeper canst thou sink?"

"Are you asking me or the world?"

"I'm asking you, Mr. Egg Embezzler."

"Oh. What was the question again?"

Funny, I couldn't remember the question either. Oh well. "The point is, you should be ashamed of yourself. For that, Drover, you can spend the next hour standing in the corner."

"Oh drat."

"Don't argue with me. Go to your room, put your nose in the corner, and say the following five hundred times: 'Only a chicken would steal an egg from his friend.' "

"Only a chicken . . . gosh, Hank, what if I can't remember all that?"

G.L.Holmes

"This afternoon, I'll give you a test to make sure you memorized it. If you flunk, then you will have crossed over the line between Serious Trouble and Very Serious Trouble. I wouldn't want to speculate on the consequences of that."

"Oh darn. Well, if I admit I ate your eggs, would you let me off without any punishment?"

"Negative. There's no plea bargaining on this ranch—not while I'm in charge and not when I've been looted by my own employees. Now go, and shame on you for a whole hour."

Drover hung his head and went padding down to the gas tanks. I watched the little mutt and hoped the punishment wasn't too severe. I only wanted to break his bad habits, not his spirit.

There are times, up here at the top, when a guy is tempted to soften his position on crime and punishment. But part of being a cowdog and a Head of Ranch Security lies in being just a little tougher than your average run of dogs.

Drover was the one with egg on his face, and now the foot was on the other shoe.

CHAPTER

4

BACON GREASE OVER BURNED TOAST MAKES A LOUSY BREAKFAST

Once Drover had left to go serve his time in jail, I turned my attention back to the scene before me.

There was Greedygut the Cat, eating my juicy bacon ends. As you may know, cats don't have a real good set of chewing teeth. Their teeth are more like spikes or needles—better for inflicting pain on innocent children than the teeth of a dog, but not as good for crushing bones or chewing meat.

In other words, I still had some hope that Pete would choke on my bacon. Stranger things have happened in this old world. If you've ever watched a cat eating, you know

33

that they often yowl while they chew. Also, they don't chew their food twenty-one times. They'll hit it four, five, or six times, then try to swaller it whole—yowling and growling at the same time.

And sometimes they choke.

I didn't wish Pete any bad luck, but if he had strangled himself on my bacon, he would have improved the world and served the cause of justice—also saved some juicy bacon ends for certain observers whose names we don't need to mention.

I waited and watched and hoped. The longer I waited and watched and hoped, the more I began to realize that this would not be a lucky day for the ranch, for the cat devoured my breakfast and didn't choke.

At that point in my career, I began looking around for secondary options, such as the two pieces of burned toast lying on the ground before me. I sniffed them. I took one of them in my mouth and gummed it around before spitting it out.

Whether you gum it or chew it or sniff it, burned toast remains basically burned toast.

But just then, I saw Sally May come out of the house with an orange juice can in her hand. She walked past the cat, who was now licking his hind leg with long strokes of his tongue, and proceeded to the south corner of the fence. She leaned across the fence and poured the contents of the orange juice can out on the ground.

Hmm. Why would Sally May be pouring orange juice out on the ground? That didn't make sense. Something strange was going on here, and I needed to check it out.

I went slipping down the fence. Sally May saw me. I stopped.

"No, Hank. It's just bacon grease. It's messy, and it'll make you sick if you eat it. Now go on."

Oh. Bacon grease. Hmm, yes. I could smell it now. Smelled pretty good. Smelled VERY good. Bacon grease may not be exactly the same as bacon, but at a distance one smells about as good as another.

I waited for Sally May to go back into the house. Little Alfred had come out by then and she told him not to get dirty because the kinfolks would be arriving in an hour. Then she went inside.

I slipped back to the spot where I had left the two pieces of charred toast, picked one up in my enormous jaws, glanced around to make sure Sally May wasn't looking, and made my

G. L. Holmes

way south down the fence. The further I went, the stronger that bacon smell became. By the time I reached the spot, I could almost taste it.

Now, it didn't look all that great, I'll have to admit that. When you pour cold bacon grease out on the ground, it looks like something you wouldn't want to eat. But the aroma . . . that's the important thing. Looks ain't everything in this old world.

See, I had worked out this very clever strategy in my mind. Listen to this. If a guy is denied real bacon and is left with nothing to eat but burned toast, he can sop the toast in the grease. While making efficient use of the resources at hand, he also fools his taste buds by making them think he's eating bacon, see.

Pretty shrewd. No cat in history has ever come up with a plan that good.

Well, I took one last glance around to make sure that the, uh, Kitchen Police weren't watching, then I dropped the toast right into the middle of the brown blob . . . into the bacon grease, I should say. I oozed it around, flipped it over, and let the other side soak up . . .

You know, that stuff smelled so wonderful that my mouth began to water. It's hard to express a dog's deep yearning for bacon. I couldn't remember the last time I'd experienced the savage delight of gobbling bacon, nor could I remember a single time in my long and glorious career when I had had at my disposal all the bacon I wanted or could eat.

I postponed the first bite as long as I could. I mean, that's part of the fun of eating—knowing you've got the goodies there in front of you but forbidding yourself from diving into it.

I sniffed it. I licked my chops. I drooled over it. I rehearsed that first bite over and over in my mind. I was just about ready to begin the procedure when I heard a voice.

"You'd better not eat that bacon grease, Hankie. It'll make you sick."

That was Pete. He was sitting on the other side of the fence, purring, twitching the end of his tail, and staring at me with his big cattish eyes.

"Oh yeah? Who says?"

"Me. And Sally May."

"Sally May's opinion carried some weight around here until you started quoting her, and that just about ruined it."

"Truth is truth, Hankie, regardless of who says it."

"Oh yeah? Well, I've got one better for you.

38

Truth is truth until it comes from the mouth of a cat. There's no truth so true that a cat can't twist it into a falsehood."

He blinked and smiled. "Well, if I felt that way about it, Hankie, I'd eat all that bacon grease."

"Would you? That's very interesting, cat, because that's just what I'm fixing to do." I chuckled and gave him a wink. "You see, kitty-kitty, I understand your little scheme. You think I'll do the opposite of anything you say, right? You tell me to eat all the bacon grease, I eat none of it, I walk away and leave it all for you, right?"

"I was just trying to be helpful, Hankie."

"Oh Pete, it hurts me to see you slipping. This game of yours is old and tired. I mean, okay, maybe it worked once or twice, but that was years ago. Life goes on, cat. You can't toot your own horn if you've only got one string on your fiddle."

"You're mixing your metaphors, Hankie."

"No, I'm mixing business with pleasure. It's my business to beat you at your own shabby games, and it's a pleasure to do it. Now, if you'll just stand back and observe, I'll begin the procedure. Before your very eyes, you'll see me devour the toast in three bites, then lick up the remaining grease until nothing remains, not even a spot.''

"You'll get sick."

I laughed in his face. "You're about to see one of the most experienced pot-lickers in Ochiltree County do his stuff. I mean, what I don't know about pot-licking hasn't even been tried yet, so stand back and study your lessons. Ready? Aim! Bonzai!''

I dived into the middle of that piece of toast. The procedure went off without a hitch. Within seconds, I had that piece of toast reduced to molecules (those are the basic building blocks of the universe, if you'd care to make a note of it), and true to my prediction, I did it in three bites.

Pete watched in sheer amazement. I'm sure he had never seen such an exhibition of brute skill.

I must admit that swallering the molecules of toast turned out to be no ball of wax, for some of the molecules still had the texture of burned toast. In other words, they scraped and scratched on the way down. But a little scraping and scratching has never scared me away from a good meal.

Upon completion of Step One of the procedure, I entered into Step Two. True to my prediction once again, I completely demolished the glob of bacon grease on the ground, licked it to the bare dirt and even managed to get some of the bare dirt in with the grease, can't say it tasted so good, I've never cared much for dirt, but what the heck, there's a price for everything.

The entire procedure, including Steps One and Two, required something less than one minute. I turned to Pete and gave him a smirk.

"What do you say now, cat? How does it feel to lose a big one?"

Before he could answer, Little Alfred, age three years and some odd months, came up behind him, grabbed him by the tail and made a wagon of him. Or maybe it was a plow, since Pete had his front claws out and did a pretty impressive job of plowing up the yard as he was being dragged around.

Little Alfred is hard on cats. That's one thing I've always admired about him. Fine kid, that Alfred.

Well, this was an unexpected pleasure. It isn't often that I can take time out of my busy schedule and watch someone else tormenting the cat. I drifted over to the yard gate, where I had a good view, and sat down to watch the show.

I loved it. You should have seen Pete's eyes. And his ears, yes, that was delicious too, had 'em pinned down and he was yowling and scowling and . . .

I burped. It just kind of snuck out.

Anyways, there was Little Alfred making the sounds of a tractor and pulling his cat-plow across the . . .

I burped again. Also noticed an unusual feeling in my, well, in the region between my lower ribs and . . . in the vicinity of my stomach, you might say, and . . . you know, all at once I didn't feel like a million dollars. It was closer to $9.95.

Anyways, Little Alfred and Pete plowed up the south side of the yard, and all at once I didn't feel worth a flip. I could hear some kind of strange noise coming from my innards—pretty muchly the sound you'd expect if you'd just eaten a couple of panthers and they'd started fighting. 'Course, I hadn't eaten any wildcats, only . . .

All at once the thought of bacon was less exciting than I'd ever thought possible. In fact, I decided that . . . I didn't want to think about bacon at that particular moment, and maybe never again for the rest of my life.

I didn't want to smell bacon either, but the

smell of bacon filled my nostrils. Oozy, drippy, greasy, smelly, stinky, oily bacon. Yuck!

I never did care much for bacon. It's too greasy for me. And once you get some stinky bacon grease on the hairs around your mouth, the smell stays with you and all you can smell is bacon, and I can't stand the smell of greasy, oily . . .

Right then and there, I took a solemn oath never to eat bacon again, nor bacon grease, nor burned toast, nor dirt. In fact, I took a solemn oath never to eat *anything* again, ever.

Fellers, I was sick, and I mean SICK. If the Angel of Death had come calling for me at that moment, I would have either jumped into his arms or throwed up, I couldn't tell which.

CHAPTER

5

WAS IT MY FAULT THAT SHE TRIPPED OVER ME AND TWISTED HER DADGUM ANKLE?

It was a real pity that I got sick at that particular moment, because the show in the back yard got better and better.

After using Pete for a plow, Little Alfred turned on the water hose and started irrigating him. I guess you know about cats and water. They don't get along. Old Pete had his ears pinned down, had a disgusted look on his face, and he was making a sound like a police siren.

On a better day, I would have considered this good wholesome entertainment. On a better day, I would have had something besides bacon on my mind. But this wasn't a better day.

I curled up in a ball in front of the yard gate and tried to think of anything but food. I tried it all—birds, rainbows, butterflies, pretty flowers. No luck. They all came out smelling like bacon grease.

Well, whilst I was there, listening to the cement mixer in my stomach, the back door burst open and Sally May came out, her housecoat flying in the breeze and the west side of her hair up in pink curlers.

"Alfred, oh Alfred! You're covered with mud and shame on you for being mean to the cat, and the company's going to be here any minute and the water pump quit working and we don't have any water pressure and I can't clean your daddy's ring around the bathtub and here you are wasting water and being mean to the cat!"

She marched over to my little pal and gave him a swat on the behind. He squalled. Then she bent over to rescue her waterlogged pet, and he being your typical dumb, ungrateful cat, hissed and scratched her, so she booted him across the yard and called him a name I'd never heard before.

Judging by the tone of her voice, I would

G. L. Holmes

47

guess that meant something besides Sweetie Pie.

It was a good kick too. When she got riled, old Sally May could be dangerous. Not only could she throw a rock, but she made a pretty good hand at booting cats. I was impressed—also glad that I was outside the yard and out of her range.

Well, she was definitely stirred up about Little Alfred's muddy clothes and the ring around the bathtub and being late for the relatives, who were coming for the Thanksgiving holiday.

She stormed over to the hydrant and turned off the water. Then she looked down at Little Alfred. His lower lip stuck out about two inches and he didn't look too happy about the state of the world.

"Your grandmother is going to be here any minute now, with two of your cousins, and you pick this time, of all times, to play in the mud. Just look at you!"

Little Alfred aimed his lip at her and stood on his tip-toes and said, "Dummy."

Uh oh. That was a big mistake. The boy should have kept his mouth shut. Even I could have told him that. For calling his mother a dummy, he got another swat on the behind.

He squalled, and we heard no more of that dummy business.

"Now you take those filthy clothes off right this minute and I'll have to clean you up all over again and I hope you haven't run all the water out of the pressure tank and . . ." She glanced at her watch. Her eyebrows flew straight up. "Oh my stars! They'll be here any minute!"

While Little Alfred pealed off his muddy clothes, Sally May made a dash to the water well, which was up the hill about ten yards west of the house. To get there, she had to go out the yard gate.

If you recall, I was curled up on the other side of the gate, hovering between sickness and death.

She hit that gate with a full head of steam. Maybe she didn't see me on the other side. Surely, if she'd seen me there, she wouldn't have opened the gate in such a way that it would hit me in the nose, but that's what she did.

With a wild look in her eyes, the unrollered half of her hair flying around on her head, and her housecoat sticking straight out behind her, she stepped in the middle of my back, tripped, stumbled, got up, turned back to me and screamed, "GET OUT OF THE GATE, YOU MORON, MY MOTHER-IN-LAW IS GOING TO BE HERE IN FIVE MINUTES!!"

HUH?

Well, you know me. I can take a hint. I jacked my diseased body up off the ground, moved a full six inches to the west, and collapsed again.

I wouldn't have done that for just anybody. But for Sally May, it was the least I could do.

She opened the lid on the well house, said something to the snakes and spiders and waterdogs down at the bottom, hit the reset button on the pump, and came charging back down the hill.

Halfway down the hill, she looked up and saw Little Alfred. He was standing buck-naked in the flowerbed, painting his tummy with mud and watering her flowers—without the garden hose.

"ALFRED! GET OUT OF THAT . . ."

Well, I was just lying there, minding my own business and trying to recover from the bacon poisoning. And, as I've pointed out, I had moved out of the gate, as she had requested.

Or, to put it another way, I had pretty much-ly moved out of the gate. I think she could have missed me if she had been paying attention to her business.

Don't get me wrong. I'm not criticizing Sally May. Over the years, she and I have had our differences of opinion, so to speak, and our relationship has had its ups and downs—more downs than ups, I would say. But basically I'm a loyal dog. I try not to find fault with my master or his wife.

What I'm driving at is that Sally May came zooming down the hill, stepped right in the middle of my stomach, stumbled, twisted her ankle, and went crashing into the fence.

Let's get something straight before we get into the dark and bloody parts of this story. I had little or no control over the various processes of my body, which had been weakened by the toxic effects of poisoned bacon grease.

I knew, in the stillness of my heart, that this was the wrong time for my body to purge itself of the deadly poisons, and I would have gladly chosen a different time and place, had I been given a choice.

But she had stepped right in the middle of my stomach, the very part of my body which was most inflamed and uneasy.

Before I knew it, I had staggered to my feet. My head hung low and suddenly my entire body was seized by a convulsion that began in the dark pit of my stomach and moved like a wave toward the end of my nose. My head moved up and down, three times, and then . . .

Exactly how and why I threw up in her shoe, I'll never know. It wasn't my idea. As near as I can tell, her shoe had come off when she'd taken that tumble and . . .

Did I put it there? Did I ask her to stomp on my stomach? Was it my fault that the water well quit working or that Little Alfred had painted himself with mud or that her stupid kinfolks were coming for a visit? If she didn't like her stupid kinfolks . . .

No. It wasn't my fault, but guess who got blamed for everything that had ever gone wrong in the entire ten thousand years of human history.

Me.

Okay. There we were. Once I had purged the poisons from my system, I felt much better, and at that point my concern shifted from myself to Sally May. I mean, she was leaning against the fence, moaning and holding her ankle.

Hey, my master's wife was injured and what she needed was a loyal dog to lick her in the face and, you know, to give her some encouragement. That's what I had in mind when I rushed to her side.

I was in the process of reeling out my tongue to give her a nice, juicy, healing lick on the cheek when, to my complete surprise, she grabbed me around the throat and started strangling me.

"YOU HORRIBLE DOG, YOU'VE BROKEN MY LEG AND MADE MY CHILD A SAVAGE AND RUINED MY HOLIDAY, AND NOW I'M GOING TO MURDER YOU WITH MY BARE HANDS!!"

Gulk, gasp, gurgle.

Hey, she wasn't kidding. My tongue was hanging out of my mouth and my eyeballs were about to pop out of my head when, thank goodness, her mother-in-law pulled up and saved my life.

Sally May's mouth dropped open when the car came to a stop beside us. Her grip around my throat loosened. She glanced around with glazed eyes and saw herself dressed in a housecoat, one shoe on and one shoe off, half her hair up in rollers.

Her son was running wild and naked

through the yard and chasing the cat.

And her lovely little hands were around the throat of her loyal dog.

"Oh. Why, Mom, I . . . is it already eleven o'clock?"

Grandma and the two girls stared at us with big unblinking eyes. Grandma nodded her head.

Sally May removed her hands from my throat. "I was just . . . I know this must look very . . . I'm not sure I can explain . . ."

She stood up and tried to walk on her twisted ankle. She couldn't do it without limping. Her lip quivered. Her eyes filled with tears and she burst out crying.

"Oh Mom, everything's gone wrong today! The bathtub's dirty, the water well doesn't work, my baby's running around naked, I think I've broken my leg, I've ruined the holiday, and most of all, *I hate this dog*!"

Grandma came over and put her arms around Sally May. "Now, now, don't you worry about that, dearie. I've been a mother too and you don't need to explain a thing to me. After all, I was the one who raised that husband of yours."

Sally May laughed and cried at the same time and buried her face on Grandma's shoulder.

G.L.Holmes

55

Grandma patted her on the back, then looked down at me. I whapped my tail on the ground, just to let her know that I understood too.

She kicked me in the ribs. "Get out of here, you nasty thing! See what you've done?"

HUH?

Well, hey, if that's the way she felt about it . . . I ran for my life.

CHAPTER
6

DROVER PASSES HIS TEST, BUT JUST BARELY

Instead of running to a far corner of the ranch, as most ordinary dogs would have done once they had worn out their respective welcomes, I hid in some weeds and watched what happened next.

I mean, Sally May had injured herself, right? Even though my conscience was clear on the matter, even though she had accused me of crimes I didn't commit, I was still concerned about her. And besides that, a guy never knows when someone is going to pull out some food and leave scraps lying around. Part of my job as Head of Ranch Security is keeping the place clean.

I'm kind of a fanatic about cleanliness. Nothing trashes up a place quite as badly as trash, and if that happens to include, oh, scraps of bread, baloney rings, chicken bones, pieces of hot dog—just about any of the food groups except vegetables and things that taste or smell like bacon—then so much the better.

There's nothing wrong or selfish about combining a zeal for cleanliness with an interest in food. Without food, where would we be in this old life? We'd all be going around looking for something to eat, which brings us back to my original concern: Sally May had injured her ankle, and I was worried about her.

Also hungry. I'd lost my breakfast, right? You can't expect a dog to operate on fresh air and sunshine . . . I don't want to beat the point to death but . . . okay. Sally May dried her tears and hobbled around on her bum leg, while Grandma went into the yard, scooped up Little Alfred, and hauled him into the house for a session in the bathtub.

When they came back outside, Alfred had shed most of his mud and was wearing civilized clothes again.

Grandma shook her finger in the boy's face and told him to stay the heck out of the mud, then she went over and looked at Sally May's ankle. She poked and squeezed, squinted her eyes and pooched out her lips, and finally said,

"Hun, I think we'd better take you to town and let the doctor look at this."

Sally May let out a groan. "But why did it have to happen on the day before Thanksgiving? If I ever see that dog again . . ."

She turned around and looked in my direction. I concentrated extra hard on blending into the environment, so to speak, and was prepared to run if she reached for a rock or a gun.

I didn't mind taking the blame for crimes I didn't commit, but my idea of being a nice guy stops short of getting murdered for it.

Sally May limped inside and changed her clothes, while Grandma herded all the kids into the car. Then Sally May came out again, using a mop for a crutch. Her eyes had a certain pinched quality about them when she looked off to the south, and I had a suspicion that she hadn't entirely given up the idea of strangling . . . well, ME, you might say.

"This is so embarrassing!" she said, as she scooted into the car seat, and I didn't hear the rest because she slammed the door.

I scrunched down in the weeds and didn't move a hair until they were gone and I heard the car rumble over the cattle guard. Then I stood up and took a deep breath.

I guess I shouldn't let little things bother me, but it kind of hurt me to see Sally May taking out all her sorrows and frustrations on me.

I know that's part of my job, but sometimes it's hard to take, especially when those girls hadn't left a single food scrap on the ground. I know because I went over the whole area three times. Not even a crumb. Sure was hungry. Sure could have used a crumb or a pound of hamburger.

Pete the Plow was sitting in the sun, licking his coat and trying to recover his dignity. Just for laughs, I hollered at him, asked how he'd enjoyed babysitting with Sally May's little monster.

He didn't answer, which was fine because I had better things to do than listen to a half-drownded cat.

I went down to the gas tanks and found Drover, standing with his nose pressed against the northeast angle-iron leg of the gas tanks. He was mumbling something.

"All right, son, it's examination time. I presume you've been studying your lessons?"

"Sure have, Hank, and I'm bored."

"Don't worry about it. Anybody who had spent the last half-hour with you would have been bored."

"So it's not just me?"

"Not at all. It's a perfectly natural reaction. But let me remind you, Drover, that this was punishment. I didn't send you down here to be frivolous."

"What does 'frillivous' mean?"

"The word is *frivolous,* and it means silly, unbusinesslike, unprofessional, greedy, self-centered, disrespectful, discourteous, disobedient, irreverent, and basically stupid."

"Gosh, that's quite a word."

"Indeed it is, and it wouldn't hurt you to remember it."

"Yeah, and then I wouldn't forget it."

"Exactly. I think you'll find, Drover, that a few fancy words, sprinkled here and there into your sentences, would help break the monogamy of your conversation."

"Gosh. What happens when you break your mahogany?"

"You either fix it or it stays broke."

"Don't they paint mahogany sometimes?"

"Sometimes they do, but plywood is much cheaper. How did we get on the subject of plywood?"

"I don't know. We were talking about big words."

"Yes, that's true. Plywood is a big word,

Drover, and you should try to sprinkle it into your conversation more often. Who knows, you might fool someone."

"Okay. You seen any plywood this morning?"

"Why do you ask?"

"Just trying to fool you."

I couldn't help chuckling at that. "Drover, if you really and truly want to fool Hank the Cowdog, you should bring camping gear, because it could take you weeks or even months. Now, where were we?"

"Plywood."

"Exactly. Plywood. Hmmm. I seem to have lost my train of thought."

"Can I take my nose out of the corner now?"

"Negative, unless you can pass a very thorough and difficult examination, and I have my doubts about that."

"Oh gosh. I've got a crick in my neck from holding my nose in the corner."

"I'm sorry to hear that, Drover, but I hope you understand that crickets have no bearing on this case. It doesn't matter how many crickets you've seen, or think you've seen. No amount of crickets can excuse your behavior."

"Hank, I've been down here so long, I don't even remember what I did."

"You stole my scrambled eggs and left me with nothing to eat but two pieces of burned toast and half a gallon of poisoned bacon grease."

"Really?"

"Yes. And I, being a kind and trusting soul, ate them and came within inches of dying a horrible death. All because of your greedy and selfish behavior. I hope you're ashamed of yourself."

"I hope so too, 'cause I sure want to get out of here."

"Are you ready to take your examination?"

"Oh, I guess—if you promise not to make it too hard."

"I'm not in a position to promise anything, Drover, except that you will get a fair trial."

"Does that mean we can't cheat?"

"That's exactly what it means. Cheaters never win, Drover, and chinners never weep. Are you ready for the first question?"

"I guess so."

"All right, here is the first question, which is also the only question. Should you fail to answer the question, you will be confined to your room for the rest of your life. In other words, don't choke under the pressure."

He made an odd sound, as though he were choking on something.

"Ready? Here we go. All right, Drover, what was it that I told you to repeat five hundred times?"

"It was a sentence. One sentence."

"That is correct. Now, repeat that alleged sentence, word for word."

"Can you give me a hint?"

"No. I'm not allowed to give any help whatsoever."

"I bet you forgot too."

"Don't be absurd."

"Was it something about zebras?"

"No. Chickens."

"Oh yeah, I remember now. Here we go: Don't count your chickens before they cross the road."

"Incorrect. I'll give you one last chance."

"Oh darn." He thought about it. "Okay, I've got it now: A chicken in the pot is worth three birds in the bush."

"No. One last chance."

He rolled his eyes and twisted his face around. "Okay, let's try this one: If you eat scrambled eggs for breakfast, the chickens will come home to roost.''

"That's close, Drover, but I'm afraid . . ."

All at once he started jumping up and down and whirling around in circles. "Oh Hank, I've got it now, I've got it!"

"Get your nose back in the corner. You haven't passed the test yet." He did as he was told. "All right, settle down, relax, get control

G.L. Holmes

of yourself. For the absolute last time, what is the answer?"

"The answer is: Only a chicken would lay an egg on the head of a friend. That's it, Hank! I got it!"

I ran that answer through my data banks. It checked out.

"Congratulations, Drover. You've passed the examination and you're now a free dog."

"Boy, that was tough."

"Yes, but I don't need to remind you that when the going gets tough . . ." Suddenly, I heard a whinney. "Did you just whinney?"

"When?"

"No, *whinney.*"

"Whinney?"

"Just now. I could have sworn that I heard a . . ." There it was again. "Yes, I did hear a whinney."

Drover rolled his eyes around. "I didn't know weenies could talk."

"Not a weenie, you dunce. A WHINNEY, the sound a horse makes."

"Oh. No, it wasn't me."

"I know that, Drover."

"Then how come you asked?"

"Because . . . never mind. The point is that my very sensitive ears have picked up the sound of a horse in the home pasture."

"I didn't think there were any horses in the home pasture."

"Exactly my point." I pushed myself up on all-fours. "And that means, Drover, that we have a new case to investigate: The Case of the Mysterious Whinney In The Home Pasture. Come on, we'd better check this thing out."

And with that, we went dashing away from the comfort and security of the gas tanks, on a course that would take us into a new adventure—and no small amount of danger.

C H A P T E R

7

TUERTO, THE ONE-EYED KILLER STUD HORSE

I don't get along well with horses, just don't like 'em and never have.

For one thing, horses have this snooty, superior attitude. They seem to think they're just a little better than the rest of us. I could take you over to the horse pasture right this minute and show you several horses that fit that description: Casey, Happy, Popeye, Deuce, Calipso, Frisco, Sinbad, Macho, Chief, Bonny Bonita, and that smart-alecky little Cookie mare.

Even Lightning, the Shetland pony, thinks he's hot stuff.

What is particularly galling about horses is that, given the slightest opportunity, they will chase a dog. In other words, they not only pretend to be superior, but they will try to prove it.

If there's anything more annoying than pretense, it's reality. And anything that weighs a thousand pounds and bites, kicks, and stomps must be considered reality.

We cowdogs are trained in the techniques of gathering, herding, and moving livestock, don't you see. These techniques are accepted and respected by cattle, sheep, goats, chickens, and hogs.

In other words, we can do business with those animals. We may not like each other, but we all play by the same rules. When we dogs go to the pasture, we don't have to invent a new game every time.

But horses? No sir. They won't play the game. They make up their own game and their own rules. And they cheat. Anyway, I don't get much of a kick out of fooling with horses.

Or, to put it another way, I often get a kick out of fooling with horses, and those kicks hurt.

Anyways, I made visual contact only moments after we swooped past the front gate and zoomed out into the pasture.

"Mayday, mayday! Drover, I'm picking up a horse at ten o'clock!"

"What are you going to put him in?"

"What?"

"And we're already an hour late."

"No no, you don't understand. In combat situations, we switch over to combat terminology."

"Oh."

"Imagine that the enemy is standing on a giant clock." (I had to explain all this while we were running.)

"Okay."

"The twelve is facing due east, which means that the six is facing due west."

"And six plus twelve makes eighteen."

"Roger. Now, the enemy is located where the ten would be, if he were the little hand."

"He doesn't look very little to me."

"Roger. And that's why we say that we've spotted the enemy at ten o'clock."

"If he's the little hand, I'd hate to see the big one."

"Just forget about the hands, Drover, and concentrate on the numbers."

"I still can't see any numbers."

"You're not supposed to. It's all imaginary."

"Is that horse imaginary too?"

"Negative."

"That's what I was afraid of. Hank, is this an alarm clock?"

"Well, I'm not sure. Why do you ask?"

"I keep hearing alarm bells in my head. Do you see who that horse is?"

I throttled back to an easy gliding pace and squinted my eyes at the alleged horse and . . .

HUH?

You might recall that only hours before, High Loper had told Sally May about the neighbor's one-lawed out-eyed stud horse—that is, one-eyed outlawed stud horse, a heartless brute named Tuerto.

I had forgotten the conversation myself, else I might not have been so anxious to answer the call and enter the case. For you see, the mysterious whinney had come, not from your ordinary arrogant, cheating, back-stabbing saddle horse, which would have been bad enough —but from that same infamous one-eyed killer, Tuerto.

Had I known that, I might have chosen to explore the far west end of ranch headquarters. Or let's put it this way: No ordinary dog would have chosen to go into combat against the villain Tuerto.

But then, being ordinary has never been on my agenda, so there you are. And also, it was too late to turn back.

"Hank, my leg's starting to hurt! I'm losing speed and altitude and attitude and just about everything else!"

"You're losing courage, is what you're losing. This is no time to come up lame."

"I know. It's already ten o'clock but the machine shed's back at six o'clock, so maybe I'd better . . ."

"Stay in formation, Drover. We're going in for a look."

"I don't need to go in for a look. I can see all I can stand from here."

"Hang on, Drover, here we go!"

"Oh, my leg . . ."

We zoomed in for a look. Sure enough, it was Tuerto of the Gotch Eye. When he saw us streaking towards him, he tossed his head and stamped his right front foot. It was pretty clear at this point that he had no business in our home pasture.

"Hank to Drover, over. Confirm visual sighting at eleven o'clock."

"I thought it was only ten o'clock."

"Roger, but suspect has moved one hour to the south."

"Time sure flies when you're scared."

"Roger. Suspect has invaded our territorial territory. Prepare to initiate Growling Mode!"

"Hank, let's don't growl at him, he might think we're being unfriendly."

"That's the whole point, Roger."

"I'm Drover."

"Of course you are. Ready? Mark! We have initiated Growling Mode One and are proceeding toward the target!"

I'm sure that a lot of this technical stuff sounds pretty heavy. I mean, you've got your rogers and your modes and your coordinates and your procedures and so forth, and while it may sound complicated, it's not so bad once you get used to it.

We were pretty muchly following the procedures outlined in Chapter Seven of *The Cowdog Manual of Combat*. You might want to put that on your list of outside reading and check it out in your spare time.

I had hoped that, once we initiated Growling Mode One, the enemy would take the hint and leave. He didn't. He continued to stamp his foot and make threatening gestures with his ears, mouth, teeth, and his one good eye.

"Hank to Drover, over. Stand by to initialize Growling Mode Two!"

"Oh my gosh!"

"Ready? Mark! We have initiated Growling Mode Two! Stand by to initialize Barking Mode One."

"Hank, what's the difference between 'initialize' and 'initiate?' "

"This is no time to ask questions, Drover. You should have learned all of that in Fight School."

"Maybe I'd better go back to the machine shed and read . . ."

"Negative on the machine shed. Once you're in the soup, it's too late to read the recipe. Stand by to initiate Barking Mode One."

"You already said that once."

"No, the first time we initialized. Now we're fixing to initiate. Stand by."

"I still don't understand the difference."

"Mark and bark! We have initiated Barking Mode One. The enemy should begin showing fear at any moment."

We barked. Boy howdy, did we bark! Should have scared that horse right out of his skin but . . . well, you might say that he didn't appear to be in a state of panic. What he did was toss his head and give us a toothy grin.

"Come a leetle closer, leetle duggies, and I

weel stomp you eento the dert."

O-kay, if that's the way he wanted it, we would have to proceed with the procedure and give him the whole nine yards of Scary and Terrifying Gestures.

"Hank to Drover, over. This is getting serious."

"I was afraid of that."

"Stand by to lift hair on back of neck and hair on back of back! Ready? Mark! We have hair lift-up."

"We have a wreck, is what we have."

"Now stand by to arm tooth-lasers."

"Tooth-lasers!"

"Roger on the tooth-lasers. Stand by. Ready?"

"No."

"Mark! We have initialized tooth-lasers! All tooth-lasers armed and ready! Stand by for Attack Mode. Bearing: three-two-zirro-zirro."

"I thought it was eleven o'clock. Now he says it's thirty-two. I don't understand . . ."

"Stand by to lock on target! Three-two-one . . . Mark!"

"Drover."

"Roger."

"Hank!"

"What?"

"Who are all these people?"

"Never mind. We have locked on Target Tuerto. Stand by for attack! Ready? Charge, bonzai!"

G.L. Holmes

Even though I had reason to suspect that Drover wasn't prepared to carry out his assignment, we initiated the attack. I went in the first wave, leaving Drover to cover my flank and tail.

With my tooth-lasers blazing, I peeled off and went streaking toward Target Tuerto. Was I scared? Maybe, a little. Who wouldn't be scared of a murdering gotch-eyed stud horse? But I swallered my fear and went charging into the frey. Fray. Frei. Battle. The attack should have worked. I mean, we must have looked pretty awesome, swooping in on him that way, with all our barking and raised hair and tooth-lasers and everything. Yes, it should have worked. However . . .

I wasn't exactly prepared for his cunning maneuver. As quick as a snake, he swapped ends and fired two hoof-cannons at me. Fortunately for me and the ranch and the rest of this story, the cannon fire passed on both sides of my head, else I might not have had a head for the next two shots to pass between.

I was struck, not by the cannon fire, but by the futility of attacking a thousand-pound horse who was attacking back. I mean, one hit by them cannons of his and I would have been *spitting* tooth-lasers instead of using them.

Suddenly an old piece of cowdog wisdom came to mind: "A triumph in battle beats a moral victory, but a moral victory beats a kick in the head."

I decided to settle for a moral victory.

"Hank to Drover, over. Stand by to initiate Retreat Mode!"

I needn't have worried about Drover. He had vanished. Under the circumstances, that seemed a pretty good idea.

I initiated the Retreat Mode and also vanished, returning to home base with a moral victory under my belt and a frenzied one-eyed stud horse hot on my trail.

CHAPTER
8

TOP SECRET MATERIAL!!!!
*Children Under Twelve Not Allowed
To Read This Chapter! Caution! Danger!
Do Not Enter! Poison!*

Before we go any farther, let's get something straight.

I try to set a good example for Drover and all the little children who consider cowdogs just a little special. So what I'm getting at is this. If the little children come up to you and ask, "Did Hank the Cowdog really run from Tuerto and hide under Sally May's car?" I'd be grateful if you'd . . . well, deny it, so to speak.

I mean, there's lots of ways of fudging on a story without actually . . . there's a fine line between lying and creating a false impression . . . the little children don't have to . . . just because we know the truth doesn't mean. . . .

Tell you what let's do. We'll label this chapter TOP SECRET and make it off limits to kids under twelve. You might consider stapling the pages together or cutting them out of the book with a pocket knife. But whatever you do, don't let the kids read it.

In fact, why don't you send them to bed so we can talk this thing over in private. Go ahead, I'll wait.

Okay. All the kids gone now? Check to make sure they're in bed and asleep. Sometimes they play possum, you know. They'll pretend to be asleep, see, but then they'll sneak out of bed and put their little ears to a crack in the door and listen.

Okay. Here we go. Here's the Dreadful Truth.

I ain't real proud that I left the field of battle under what we might call hasty circumstances. Even though the enemy was deadly and dangerous, even though I managed to turn it into a moral victory, it had all the markings of a blind retreat.

Indeed, an outside observer might have said that it WAS a blind retreat and . . . all right, maybe. . . .

This is very painful, see. A dog spends his whole life trying to do the right thing, trying

82

to build up a good reputation, trying to teach the kids to be courageous and bold, and then, in just a matter of seconds, everything he's worked so hard to build up goes to pot.

Okay, let's get it over with. I ran from Tuerto because I was scared of him, and all that stuff about winning a moral victory was just fluff and soap bubbles.

I didn't just run a few feet, fellers, I went streaking all the way back to the house. Sally May's car was parked out front, and I admit that I dropped down on my belly and crawled underneath. It was at that point that I discovered Drover had gotten there first.

He gave me his usual silly grin. "Hi, Hank, what you doing here?"

"No, the real question, Drover, is what are *you* doing here, but don't bother to answer because I already know."

"You do?"

"Yes. You ran from the field of battle and left me to be mauled by a dog-eating maniac."

"No, I ran from that horse."

"That's what I'm talking about, you dope."

"Oh. Well, I sure ran, I won't deny that."

"Of course you won't. You've been caught in the act."

"Sure looks like it. Gee, I thought this was a pretty good hiding place. Did you run the horse off?"

"I uh . . . you might say that."

"Okay. Did you run the horse off?"

"In a manner of speaking, yes, I think he probably ran."

"You whipped him, huh? Good old Hank! Boy, I wish I could just go out and whip a horse any time I wanted to."

"All it takes is practice, Drover. Practice and guts and skill and brains."

"Yeah. If it wasn't for this leg of mine . . ."

"Drover, that so-called leg of yours is just a crutch."

"No, it's a real leg. See, it's hooked on up here." He pointed to his armpit.

"I think you missed the point."

"Oh."

"The point is that this so-called problem with your so-called leg is just a psychological crutch."

"That sounds pretty serious."

"Indeed it is. Only a crippled mind needs a psychological crutch, Drover, and you may have one of the most crippled minds I ever ran across."

"Gosh, thanks, Hank."

"That's nothing to be proud of. Sometimes I even think you're a hypocardiac."

"No fooling? Mom always said we were just soup hounds."

"It's possible to be both a soup hound and a hypocardiac. Both are the result of poor breeding."

"I sure like soup, I know that."

All at once I noticed that his eyes had widened to the size of small plates, and that his eyeballs had crossed. "Something's wrong with your eyes, Drover."

He opened his mouth, as if to speak, but no words came out.

"This could be another symptom of your hypocardia. Yes, of course it is. First the mind goes, then the legs, then the eyes. It's all fitting together." He moved his mouth again, and again nothing came out. "Relax, Drover, don't try to speak. You've had an attack of . . ."

"Hank, there he is again!"

"Who? What?" I tried to follow his gaze but that wasn't so easy since his eyes were crossed. "You must be seeing things, Drover. Just try to . . . HUH?"

At that point I saw one of the things he was seeing: a huge mouth armed with huge teeth. It belonged to Tuerto the Killer Stud Horse, and it appeared that he was trying to crawl under the car with us.

I bristled and growled and leaped into the air, forgetting for the moment that we were under Sally May's car, which meant that instead of leaping into the air, I leaped my head against the muffler. It hurt.

"Bark, Drover, we're under attack, this is Red Alert!"

I tuned up and went into some serious barking, while Drover crawled around in circles and squeaked. "Oh Hank, what if he gets under here with us, oh my gosh, time out, king's X, tell him not to bite!"

I could hear Tuerto's wicked voice: "Come out, duggies, come out and play weeth me. I weel bite your tails."

"Don't let him in, Hank, tell him we're not here, oh my leg . . ."

"Quit squeaking and get control of yourself! And bark."

I barked and growled and snarled and snapped. By this time it had occurred to me that a horse which stood sixteen hands at the withers couldn't possibly crawl under a car that stood only three hands at the running board.

You probably think I should have known

G. L. Holmes

that all along. Well, let me tell you something. When you see a monster mouth and two rows of monster teeth coming at you beneath a car . . . never mind.

My courage began to return and I grew bolder in my counterattack. I not only bristled and barked, but I inched forward on my belly and *bit* him on the soft part of the nose.

Hey, that got his attention. You think that big lug wasn't shocked? He jerked back and all at once we saw no more of his flappy mouth, so I crawled forward through the dirt and poked my head out from under the car and cut loose with another withering barrage of barking.

Hmm. High Loper was out there, ahorseback. He took the double of his rope and laid a stroke across Tuerto's back. That got his attention! (Course, I had already softened him up with that slash to the nose.) Tuerto snorted and pawed the air with his front hooves, and Loper laid another stroke across his back.

I barked louder than ever. No question about it, me and Loper made a dangerous team. Yes sir. We didn't fool around with these two-bit cocky hot-rod horses. We worked 'em over and sent 'em home, is what we did.

And, as you might have already guessed, Tuerto pointed himself toward the home ranch and got the heck away from us. I mean, that horse was scared.

I had my head poked out from under the car, and now that it was all over, Drover crawled up beside me. Loper looked down at us, and I gave him a big cowdog smile. I knew he was proud.

"Well, there's Laurel and Hardy, protecting my ranch," he said. (Laurel and Hardy must have been famous guard dogs.) "You kept him out from under Sally May's car, didn't you?" (Yup, we done that, all right). "Sure makes me proud that I spend thirty bucks a month on dog food." (Told you he was proud). "That's what I call throwing money down a rat hole."

He turned his horse and rode off, coiling up his rope.

I crawled out from under the car and shook the dust off my coat. Drover stayed where he was.

"Hank, what did he mean, throwing money down a rat hole?"

"You don't know, really?"

"No, don't have any idea."

I walked over to him and looked down into

his empty eyes. "It's very simple, Drover. I'll explain it to you one time and I'll expect you to remember it."

"Okay. Fire away."

"All right. Pay attention. If you knew you had a very important, very valuable rat on your ranch, and you wanted to reward him for his outstanding work, would you throw money down a skunk hole or a rat hole?"

"Let's see." He squinted one eye and chewed on his lip. "A rat hole?"

"That's correct, Drover, because rats live in . . . what?"

"Uh . . . rat holes?"

"Exactly. And skunks live . . . where?"

"Uh . . . in skunk holes?"

"Correct again. This may be a new record for you, Drover, three right answers in a row, and all in the same month. And now you understand what he was saying."

"I guess so." He crawled out and scratched his left ear. "But Hank, can I ask you one more question?"

I checked the location of the sun. "I believe we have time enough for one more question. Go ahead."

"Who were those guys you were talking to out in the pasture?"

"Guys? What guys?"

"When we were out fighting the horse, you kept calling for Mark and Roger. I never did see 'em."

Well, we needn't waste any more time with Drover's nonsense. The important thing is that, once again, we had rid the ranch of a menace and had taught Tuerto the One-Eyed Killer Stud Horse a lesson he wouldn't soon forget.

(This chapter turned out better than I expected, so if the kids want to read it, go ahead and let 'em. And don't pay any attention to that part about me being scared of Tuerto. I was misquoted, that's all.)

CHAPTER

9

SALLY MAY RETURNS
ON CRUTCHES

It must have been several hours later when I heard a car rumble over the cattle guard between the home pasture and the horse pasture.

Drover and I had spent the last of the morning and the early part of the afternoon winding down from our confrontation with Tuerto the One-eyed Killer Stud Horse. We had gone up to the machine shed and crunched some Co-op dog food, then stretched out in the sun there on the south side of the shed.

In the fall of the year, the south side of the machine shed is one of the preferred sleeping areas on the ranch. The shed takes the sting out of the north wind and that old sun warms a guy up and makes him want to stretch out and take a nap—especially if he's spent all morning fighting killer horses.

I mean, that'll wear a feller down to a nubbin about as quick as anything.

Anyway, I'd caught myself a little nap and refreshed myself and was in the process of yawning and stretching the kinks out of my back, when I heard a car rumble over the cattle guard.

Well, you know me. My ears shot up and I told Drover to prepare himself for a lightning dash up to the county road, because I suspected that our old enemy, the mailman, had just made another encroachment of our territory.

We went ripping around the east side of the machine shed and had shifted into Barking Mode One when I saw Grandma's car turn at the mailbox and start down toward the house. In the blink of an eye, I reversed all engines and slid to a stop.

"Hold it, son, shut her down! I've got a feeling that this would be a good time to hide out and become scarce."

"How come?"

I told him about Sally May's unfortunate accident, that she had twisted her ankle and had gone into town to see the doctor, and that she might not be happy to see . . . well, a certain unnamed ranch dog so soon after she had tried to strangle him.

"She tried to strangle you, no fooling?"

"That's correct, with her bare hands. I mean, that old gal may wear perfume and curl

her hair, but once she gets down in the dirt and throws a few punches, she's meaner than nine junkyard dogs with a bellyache."

"Gosh, that doesn't sound like the Sally May I know."

"Whatever you think, Drover. If you want to run the risk of getting impaled on a crutch, just go on and meet the car. But I'm warning you, she's dangerous."

"I think I'll go down and welcome her back to the ranch."

"Fine. Go say hello and we'll see what happens, but if you come back wearing a crutch through your rib cage, don't expect to get any sympathy from me."

"Okay, Hank. Here I go!"

He scampered away to meet the car, while I slipped off to the north and established an observation post amongst the pine, spruce, bodark, and Russian olive trees in the shelter belt.

The car pulled around to the back of the house, with my sawed-off, stub-tailed, pea-brained assistant scampering along behind. The doors flew open and three children jumped out—Little Alfred and his two girl-cousins. Grandma got out, went around to the passenger side, and opened the door for Sally May.

As I had predicted, her ankle was wrapped up in a big white bandage and she was on crutches. Drover went up to her, wagging his stub tail and groveling in the dirt and doing this thing he often does to make points—he lifts his lips and shows his teeth, and people just love it because they think he's smiling.

If I tried that, they'd accuse me of showing fangs and making threatening gestures. Drover does it and wins points and everybody laughs and says, "Oh, isn't he cute!"

That's okay. I never wanted to be cute anyway. But it does kind of irritate me that . . . oh well.

Sally May was smiling and seemed to be in a much better humor. She and Grandma talked about baking pies and taking the wild turkey out of the deep freeze.

This was the same wild turkey Loper had brought home a couple of weeks ago. His story, as I recall, was that the turkey had run into his pickup and broken its neck. Ho, ho. I happened to be in the back of the pickup that afternoon and I can reveal here, for the first time, the true and uncensored story.

We drove up on a group of wild turkeys along the creek, don't you see, and this being the holiday season, Loper decided that he needed one. What that turkey ran into was not the pickup but a .22 bullet, which was slightly illegal since Loper hadn't bought a hunting license that year.

I can also reveal that Loper picked the turkey down at the feed barn, stuffed all the feathers into a paper sack, and buried it in the sand along the creek. Sounds pretty suspicious, huh? Yes, indeed.

I could go even further and reveal that, while he buried the feathers, I stayed behind and, uh, stood guard over the nice, plump, juicy turkey which was hanging by a piece of baling wire from a corral post, and boy, it was a good thing that I stayed behind to guard it because, well, any old stray dog who happened along could have hopped up on his hind legs and made himself a meal—and I mean a *good* meal—on that nice, plump, tender, juicy. . . .

As I said, I *could* reveal this little episode, but I won't, for various reasons. But as you can see, there was more to the turkey story than the general public knew about. I mention it here, not because I'm one to go around blabbing, but only to point out that Old Hank isn't the only one on this outfit who is guilty of naughty behavior.

Anyway, where were we? Oh yes. Drover had tested the temperature of the water, so to speak, and had found it to be something better than ice cold, so I decided, what the heck, maybe I ought to go on down and patch things up with Sally May.

Yes, I know. She'd called me terrible names and screeched at me and tried to strangle me, but I've never been one to carry a grudge.

I mean, beneath all the hair and muscle and armor plating that a guy needs in this line of work, I'm very warm and forgiving and expressive and loving, bold and courageous and as stout as an ox, a hard worker, good with children, devilishly handsome, if you believe the ladies, and. . . .

I decided to go down and make peace with Sally May, is the basic point.

I left the shelter belt and headed down to the yard. Sally May was halfway between the gate and the back door when she glanced around and saw me coming.

The smile wilted on her mouth. Dark clouds, so to speak, gathered on her brow. Her eyes narrowed and she said, "Here comes that oaf of a dog!'' Upon hearing which I did a quick about-face and returned to the shelter belt.

That was okay with me. I have never depended on the approval of small minds for my happiness. If she wanted to play freeze-out with me, we'd just by George play freeze-out.

Time passed very slowly in the shelter belt. I got bored. I bore easily. When you're accustomed to lots of excitement and action, it's hard to adjust to the humdrum existence that ordinary dogs accept as normal. I didn't have any important cases to work on, it was just a tad too chilly for a dip in the sewer and. . . .

Ho hum. I watched the kids playing with Drover and Pete. They seemed to be having fun. Having fun has never been a big deal with me. A lot of dogs think that's what this life is all about—having fun all the time, one big party after another—and what the heck, I didn't figger it would hurt me or anybody else if I went down and had a little fun myself.

I pushed myself up, shook the grass off my coat, checked all points of the compass to make sure that Sally May wasn't lurking in the evergreens with a butcher knife, and padded down to donate my presence to the little children.

They were nice kids, after all, and they deserved a break.

C H A P T E R

10

THANK THE LORD FOR MAKING GALS!

At first I sat down beside the yard gate and watched them playing. I didn't want to appear too anxious, see. Also, I wasn't sure I wanted to get involved in playing Beauty Shop or Dress Up.

I mean, when you're Head of Ranch Security, you've got to protect your dignity. Seemed to me that Beauty Shop and Dress Up weren't exactly right for me.

Now for Drover, those games were all right. He didn't have a public image to maintain, and Pete—well, who cares about a cat anyway?

Amy, one of the girl-cousins, must have been, oh, I'd say nine or ten years old. She had hair the color of a field of ripe wheat. I'd guess Ashley's age at eight, and she had the prettiest blue eyes you ever saw, same color as the sky on a still afternoon in the fall.

We'd never had any little girls on the ranch and I wasn't sure how I'd get along with them. I stayed outside the yard and watched them dressing up Drover and Pete in doll clothes. They stuffed Drover into a pair of striped overalls and had Pete rigged up in a nightgown. They both looked goofy.

No, that wasn't my brand of fun. I had better things to do than . . . but you know, that little Ashley came out the gate and looked at me with those blue eyes and stroked me on the head and invited me into her beauty shop and. . . .

Oh what the heck, I had a few minutes to burn.

Those gals were quite a contrast to Alfred, the ornery little stinkpot, who was your typical three year old boy made of snails and rails and puppydog tails, gunpowder, lizards, toad frogs, and a dash of alligator juice.

That boy could make more noise more different ways and do it longer than anybody I'd ever come across. One minute he was a cattle truck, then he was a tractor, then he was a bulldozer, then he was a bugle or a drum or a

G.L. Holmes

chainsaw or a machine gun—just anything that made noise.

He's the only kid I ever met who could start off singing "Old MacDonald Had A Farm," switch to a chainsaw, sing "Jesus Loves Me," and then spray you in the face with his bull-dozer imitation, all in the space of two minutes.

By himself, Little Alfred could be a—how shall I put this? Better just drop it. He was Sally May's child, after all, and I had reason to suspect that she loved him.

Let's just say that Little Alfred was easier to bear when he fell under the good influence of his girl-cousins. They were giving the orders that afternoon, and their brand of play didn't require any bulldozers, bombs, or sirens.

They also told him to stop cranking my tail, which I appreciated.

I sat down in the beauty shop and smirked at Drover. "Son, if you knew how silly you look, you'd go dig a hole and bury yourself. And Kitty-Kitty looks even sillier than you do."

Pete gave me a dark glare. He wasn't enjoying Dress Up. I could tell because his ears were lying flat on his head.

Drover grinned. "Sure is fun, though. Wait

'till they fix your hair. You'll like that."

"I doubt that, son. I won't be staying long. I'm just here to check things out."

But you know what? I did kind of enjoy it. Ashley took a brush and ran it through my hair, smoothed it out with her hands, and my goodness, her little hands were just as soft and gentle as rose petals, and now and then she would look down in my face and smile and. . . .

Never thought I'd fall for blue eyes, but fellers, there was something about them eyes and her smile and the way she held my face in her hands and stroked my hair and, oh what the heck, there was worse things in the world than getting your hair rolled up in pink curlers.

Boy, she was a heart-breaker, that gal. Had the cutest little pointed nose you ever saw and red lips that were shaped like a bow and skin as smooth as whipped cream, and you know, when she put that dress on me and tied the sun bonnet under my chin, I just sat there, wagging my tail and looking up into her eyes.

Fellers, if she'd asked for the moon, I would have been on the next rocket ship to space. If she'd asked for the stars, I would have picked her a bushel basketful out of the Texas sky. If she'd asked for a song . . . well, shucks, I

would have written her one, something like
this one here.

Thank You Lord For Making Gals

Oh little boys like snakes and frogs,
They're mean to cats and puppydogs.
They'll pull your tail and twist your nose,
And drive their tractor across your toes.
They'll make you mad and they'll make
   you howl,
And make you glad for little gals.

Oh thank you Lord for making gals!
They give a boost to our morale.
This would be a sad old world
If we had frogs instead of girls.

These little donkeys we call boys
They make a mess and lots of noise.
You always know when they're close by,
They tease the girls and make 'em cry.
They're hard on clothes and break their toys,
There ain't much use for little boys.

Oh thank you Lord for making gals!
They give a boost to our morale.

This would be a sad old world
If we had frogs instead of girls.

Little boys ain't fit to keep,
They'll mess things up and make you weep.
They keep the place all torn apart,
They'll run your hose and break your heart.
They'll make you cuss and they'll make
    you growl.
And make you wish for a little gal.

Oh thank you Lord for making gals!
They give a boost to our morale.
This would be a sad old world
If we had frogs instead of girls.

So thanks again for little gals!
They'll treat you nice and be your pals.
But I swear by stars above
Watch out, or you'll fall in love!

Yes sir, watch out or you'll fall in love. That
was sure the truth. But I didn't take my own
advice. I wasn't watching out and I fell in love
with them two little gals.

Whatever they wanted to do with me, that
was just by George all right. And if they'd
wanted to take me home with 'em after the

holiday, I was ready to resign my position as Head of Ranch Security and move out.

Well, we played Dress Up and Beauty Shop for a while, then Amy went inside and brought out a little wooden table and some plastic dishes and we played Tea Party.

They had me and Drover stand up on our back legs and put our front paws on the table, see, and then Amy poured everyone a cup of "tea." (It was really milk.) I noticed that Drover was grinning at me.

"Are you grinning at anything in particular or is this your usual expression?"

"Who me? Was I grinning?"

"Yes, you were, and you still are."

"Oh, gee. I guess I've never seen you in curlers and a dress and a sun bonnet before."

"Is that so?"

"Yeah. You look kind of funny."

"I see. Well, it might surprise you to know that you look a little strange in your striped overalls."

"I do?"

"Yes, you do, and dogs who live in glass houses shouldn't call kettles black."

"Dogs who live in glass . . . okay, I'll try to remember that."

"Do that. And you might also remember

that making little girls happy is part of our job. Also that beauty knows no pain. Also that sticks and stones my break my bones, but you can just shut up.''

''That's a lot to remember.''

''You can do it, son, but if you have any trouble, just remember the 'shut up' part.''

''Oh, okay.''

Pete was being a spoil-sport about playing Tea Party, but that was no big surprise. You know these cats. They never want to do anything for anybody else, just too selfish.

He still had his ears flattened against his head and the pupils of his eyes had gotten big, and he was flicking the end of his tail and giving off that growl-siren of his. I never did care for that, and I noticed that every time I looked at him, my lips began to curl up.

Well, the gals told me and Drover to drink our tea, so I put on an impressive demonstration of how a huge enormous cowdog can lap milk out of a tiny teacup, without spilling a drop or knocking over the cup. It ain't every dog who can do that.

Whilst I was demonstrating this technique, Grandma walked out the back door and looked at us. Her face lit up and she called for Sally May.

"Sally May, grab your camera and come look at this! It's the cutest thing I ever saw."

A minute later Sally May came hobbling out the door on her crutches. Seeing her there within crutch range made me a little uncomfortable. I wagged my tail and looked the other way, hoping she wouldn't do anything rash.

I mean, Sally May armed with a rock is bad enough, but when she's packing two crutches, watch out.

Lucky for me, she smiled, even laughed. "Well my stars, is *that* my husband's dog, the same one I wanted to kill this morning? I hope you girls don't get leprosy from handling the nasty thing . . ."

I glanced around, looking for a "nasty thing." Didn't see one.

". . . and girls, we'll want to go straight to the washing machine with those doll clothes when you get done." She looked at us and shook her head. "I'll swear, Mom, between kids and dogs, a poor woman never knows which way her feelings might go."

"Isn't that the truth!"

Sally May held the crutches under her arms and brought up the camera. She told us to smile and hold still. I held still but didn't smile. I leave all the smiling stuff for Drover. I don't mind playing Dress Up and Tea Party, but I don't intend to smile about it. That wouldn't be dignified.

The ladies went back inside to work on their punkin pies, and I finished lapping milk out of my teacup. Down towards the bottom, the cup started moving around the table and I had to move with it. This brought me closer to Pete, and he made the mistake of hissing at me.

Well, you know me. There's some things I can tolerate and some things I can't. No cat hisses at Hank the Cowdog and gets by with it. My lips curled. I bared my fangs and growled.

Pete fired up that yowl of his, hissed again, and popped me on the nose with his claws. Hey, that was the wrong thing to do. I was fixing to pulverize. . . .

Lucky for Kitty-Kitty, Amy and Ashley made a dive for me, grabbed me around the neck, and somehow managed to prevent my highly conditioned body from flying like an artillery shell right into the middle of the dumb cat. Saved his life, is what they did, 'cause I was all set to clean his plow.

Well, Kitty-Kitty had been looking for an excuse to escape anyhow, he being a kill-joy and a spoil-sport, and he went bounding across the yard, ducked under the fence, and headed out into the pasture—taking the night-gown with him.

The girls turned me loose and ran after him, out into the pasture.

It was at that point that Drover said, "Gosh, I hope Tuerto isn't around."

"Don't be absurd. After that scare me and Loper threw into him, I doubt that we'll ever see. . . ."

HUH?

Unless I was badly mistaken, my sensitive ears had just picked up the sound of horse's hooves.

Coming from the east.

In the home pasture.

CHAPTER

11

A FIGHT TO THE DEATH WITH THE KILLER STUD HORSE

I turned to Drover. "Do you hear something?"

"What?"

"I said, do you hear something?"

"Well, I hear your voice, and birds, and a war going on."

"That's not a war, you imbecile, that's Little Alfred playing trucks. Do you hear horse's hooves?"

"Well, let's see." He cocked his head. "No, I don't . . . oh yeah, I do, sure do, sounds just like . . . oh my gosh, Hank, do you reckon it could be. . . ."

"Yes, of course! At last the pieces of the

puzzle are falling into place, for you see, Drover, there are no other horses in the home pasture. It's Tuerto the Killer Stud Horse!"

"Oh my gosh, he might hurt those girls!"

"Not while we still have a breath left in our respective bodies, Drover."

"I'd kind of like to save my breath, and anyway this old leg is starting to act up on me again and. . . ."

"Come on, son! This is Red Alert and Code Three, all rolled into one. Stand by for blast-off! Stand by to initiate attack formation! Stand by for Heavy Duty Barking Mode!"

"I'll sure bark, Hank, but . . ."

"Ready? Blast-off! Hit the grit, let's go, stay behind me and stand by for further orders!"

"Well . . ."

I went zooming across the yard, past the iris bed, past that big hackberry tree there on the south side of the house. When I came to the yard fence, I leaped upward and outward and became airborne.

Behind me, I heard Drover call out, "Hank, I don't think I can jump the fence! It's too tall and my leg. . . ."

There wasn't time to fool around with Drover. Up ahead, I could see Tuerto pounding across the pasture, his mane and tail flying in the wind, his gotch-eye a reflection of his gotch-heart.

He was heading straight for my girls, who had caught up with Pete and were trying to get him out of the nightgown.

I began barking. "Run, girls, run! I'll cover for you, run for the house!"

Instead of running, they looked up, saw the horse pounding down on them, and froze—the very worst thing they could have done. But Pete, who was always quick to size up a situation and take good care of Pete, suddenly turned into a hissing, spitting, yowling little buzzsaw.

He broke away from the girls and went sprinting for the nearest tree.

Tuerto was getting closer now. He began to buck and snort. He pinned back his ears and showed his teeth and headed straight for the poor frightened little girls.

My original battle plan had called for me to initiate a defensive maneuver—to draw Tuerto's attention to me, in other words. I had hoped to distract him, using my amazing quickness and speed to stay out of range of his hooves while the girls made a run for the house.

But when I barked and tried to draw his

attention, he only laughed and kept going. "No, leetle duggie, I don't want you. I want these gerls!"

I had to scratch that plan. I was in the process of trying to come up with another when I heard Ashley scream—little Ashley of the clear blue eyes, little Ashley of the rose-petal hands. Then Amy let out a scream.

Well, hey, there's a time to make stragedy and there's a time to fight for what's right and good in this world, never mind the consequences.

When I was convinced that Tuerto wasn't going to let up on his attack, I abandoned all plans and went after him. No one-eyed stud horse was going to beat up on MY girls!

I got to him just seconds before he reached them, and I gave him a pile driver attack that he couldn't ignore.

I didn't fool around, fellers, I went for his throat. When they out-weigh you by a thousand pounds, you don't go for hocks or flanks or noses. You go for something they can't live without.

I went flying through the air and sank my teeth into his throat. That shut him down. All at once he wasn't thinking about beating up on a couple of little girls, 'cause he had fifty-seven pounds of killer cowdog chewing on his vital parts.

He slid to a stop, reared up on his back legs, pawed the air with his front hooves, and gave his head a mighty toss. I held on as long as I could and then he threw me off.

I hit the ground and bounced right back, and before he could strike the girls, I put myself in the middle, and there I stood, bristled up like a boar coon, growling, barking, showing fangs, giving him the whole nine yards of threatening gestures.

By this time the girls had gotten over their shock and were cheering me on. "Get him, Hank! Bite him! Go away, you mean old horse!"

Well, hey, I was proud to have someone cheering me on, but I wanted them girls to make a run for the yard, while I was still able to fight Tuerto off of them. I guess the little scamps didn't want to leave me there alone.

Just then, Grandma came out on the front porch and screamed. She told the girls to run for the house, and she came out in her long dress and grandma shoes, yelling, "Scat! Hike! Go away!"

Tuerto got a laugh out of that, and while he was yucking it up, I made another dive for his throat. Bull's eye! And while he was slinging me around, the girls made a run for the house. Grandma met them at the gate, gathered them up, pushed them into the yard, and slammed the gate shut.

G. L. Holmes

Then Tuerto turned to me. Our eyes met—my two and his one. "Ah leetle duggie, you spoil my fun so much. Now I must keel you. Never have I keeled a dog who was wearing a dress."

I had forgotten about the dress. "Well, this is your big chance, Gotch-Eye."

"Eet weel not take long, you weel see. One queek heet with my hoof and you weel be no more."

"Oh yeah?" That was the best reply I could think of. Oftentimes you think of the snappier replies the next day.

I hadn't planned to get myself drawn into a fight. I mean, I had gotten my gals out of the combat zone and finished my rescue mission and was ready to call it a day.

But just then Grandma ventured back outside, picked up a rock and threw it at Tuerto. "You hateful thing, go away from here this very minute!"

He made a move towards her. She squealed, snatched her dress up to her knees, and sprinted back into the yard, her grandma shoes clacking on the gravel.

Just for a second there, I let my attention lapse. I was watching Grandma instead of Tuerto, and he seized on the opportunity.

Before I knew it, he had clubbed me over the head with a hoof.

I saw stars and moons and checkers and flashes and colored lights. I was stunned. I knew I had to run but my legs had turned to water. My knees gave out. For a moment I couldn't move, and he hit me again, this time with both hooves.

I could feel myself being pulled into a dark wave, but then I heard my girls calling my name.

"Hank! Hank! Get up before he hurts you! Run!"

I fought against the darkness. I pushed myself up on all-fours and weaved from side to side. I tried to growl and noticed that blood was dripping from my mouth.

Tuerto went up on his back legs and sent down another storm of hooves. One got me on the ear. It hurt so bad, I began to wonder how I would look with only one ear.

But then I fought back. I got a bite on his upper leg and bore down. He shook me loose, but I came away with a piece of skin and the taste of blood. I couldn't tell if it was my blood or his, but it definitely was his skin.

Well, that made him mad. He went up on his

121

back legs again and loaded up for another round.

"RUN, HANK, RUN!"

"Honey child, I'd be glad to run, but these old legs have just quit me."

I collapsed and watched the hooves come down. I felt the first one and heard the bone in my back leg snap like a twig. After that, I didn't feel a thing and heard no more.

The great cold darkness moved around me and began to carry me away.

12

HAPPY ENDING AND ALSO THE CASE OF THE FLYING PUNKIN PIE

When I awoke, I was in Dog Heaven. I saw clouds floating past and two angels standing over me. I was a little surprised that I had made it into heaven without an argument at the gate.

I mean, I had always tried to live a good life and be a good dog, but I was also aware that I had, uh, certain blemishes on my record—such as the time I had eaten the T-bone steaks Sally May had left out to thaw, the time I had. . . .

Speaking of Sally May, *there she was,* standing above me and . . . HUH? *Holding a shot-*

123

gun? Holy smokes, this wasn't Dog Heaven! I'd gone to the Other Place!

That sort of confirmed my worst nightmares, that I would end up in Doggie Hell and find out that the place was run by Sally May instead of the Devil. All at once I regretted every naughty thing I'd ever done and wished that I could apply for another assignment.

But wait! If I had landed in Doggie Hell, what were those two angels doing there? My head began to clear and my eyes began to focus, and I recognized the angels: Ashley and Amy. Then I glanced around and saw Little Alfred and Grandma. And Drover.

"Hi Hank, how you doing?"

"Swell. How did you get here?"

"I don't know. Been here for years. That horse sure beat you up, didn't he?"

"Horse? What horse?" Then it all came back and the pieces of the puzzle fell into place. "Where's Tuerto?"

"Oh, he couldn't stay. Sally May peppered him with the shotgun and he went home."

"Bless Sally May's heart. She not only saved my life, she saved me from a fate worse than death. In other words, I'm still alive."

"Sure looks that way to me."

My head was lying in Amy's lap and Ashley

G.L. Holmes

was stroking my neck—not such a bad deal, in spite of a few aches and pains.

Grandma cleared her throat. She had a very serious expression on her face. "Well, Sally May, you have a dog with a broken leg. What are you going to do with him?"

"I don't know, Mom. What would you do?"

Grandma sighed and looked up at the sky. "Honey, I'd probably do what I've done before—load the worthless rascal up, take him to town, get him patched up, cry over the vet bill, and spend the rest of my life wondering why I did it."

Sally May nodded. "That sounds like something I might do."

"He *did* save the girls."

"Yes, he did."

"Shall I bring the car around?"

"There's nothing for this in our budget."

"I have a little extra this month. I'll contribute to the Hank Fund."

"But Mom, he's such a scoundrel!"

"I know. Shall I bring the car around?"

Sally May closed her eyes, shook her head, and heaved a sigh. "I guess there's nothing else to do. Yes, bring the car around. Girls, get some towels out of the bathroom. Alfred, please stop putting dirt in your shoes."

Grandma went to get her car and the kids ran up to the house. That left me and Sally May alone. Made me feel mighty uncomfortable. She kept staring down at me and shaking her head. Her lips moved but no words came out.

Then she laid her crutches aside and sat down on the ground beside me. She laid my head in her lap and sang me a little song. Here's how it went.

A Fundamental Disagreement

We seem to have a problem relating, you
    and I,
We seem to have a problem, seeing eye to
    eye.
We seem to stand a world apart on almost
    everything.
It's a fundamental disagreement.

I know you think I'm fussy about my yard
    and home,
You probably think I'm wicked, my heart is
    made of stone.
You just don't seem to understand or even
    really try,
It's a fundamental disagreement.

Oh Hank, if you would just shape up!
Oh Hank, if you could take a hint!
Oh Hank, you love the septic tank!
Why can't you change your ways and try to
be good?

I could be a lot more patient if you were
just less crude.
Sometimes I think God put you here to test
my fortitude.
And if you'd leave my cat alone and not
corrupt my child,
We have a fundamental disagreement.

I'd rather not be near you when you've just
fought a skunk
I've tried it several times before and, Hank,
you've really stunk.
My nose is very sensitive, I guess that's at
the root
Of our fundamental disagreement.

Oh Hank, if you would just shape up!
Oh Hank, if you could take a hint!
Oh Hank, you love the septic tank!
Why can't you change your ways and try to
be good?

I guess we'll take you to the doctor and put
  you through the mill.
We'll get your broken leg fixed, and then
  we'll pay the bill.
I can't explain my reasoning, it doesn't
  make much sense.
It's a fundamental disagreement.

A woman has an instinct for keeping things
  alive.
When we see a creature suffering, our spirits
  take a dive.
But, Hank, you strain my instincts and put
  them to the test.
It's a fundamental disagreement.

Oh Hank, if you would just shape up!
Oh Hank, if you could take a hint!
Oh Hank, this trip will us cost a mint!
Why can't you change your ways and try to
  be good?
Become a nicer dog and do what you
  should?
I'd like you better if you just understood.

While she sang to me, I looked up into her
eyes and gave her my sincerest loyal dog ex-

pression and whapped my tail. I made solemn promises to shape up, to take a hint, to stay out of the overflow of the septic tank, and to leave her stupid cat alone forever and ever.

When she was done, she looked down at me and rubbed me behind the ears. "Hank, you're such a bad dog, and I guess you'll never change."

Oh no, she was wrong about that. I had taken the Pledge, I had turned over a new leaf, I had begun a new life. Things were going to be different this time.

"But I'll say this for you, Hank McNasty. You came through when we needed you today. You were a brave dog. I'll try to remember that in the future when you mess up again."

Hey, there wasn't going to be a next time. This was a new deal. We were starting all over with a clean slate. No more mess-ups for this dog. She'd see.

Grandma pulled the car around front. They laid a towel across the back seat and placed me on top of it. Sally May and the girls rode in the back with me, and thank goodness, they put Little Mr. Wiggleworm in the front with Grandma.

My old leg was pretty well messed up and

G.C. Holmes

every time we went across a cattle guard, I felt needles of pain shooting all over my body. I tried to be brave and tough, but now and then I couldn't help whimpering.

But you know, every time I whimpered, Sally May and the girls scratched me and rubbed me and patted me and whispered soft things in my ears, and shucks, by the time we reached the vet clinic, I had just about decided that I should bust a leg more often. It would have been okay with me if Grandma had decided to drive on up to Kansas.

Now, when they carried me inside the clinic, that wasn't much fun. It hurt. Oh, how it hurt! And I admit that I growled at the doctor and tried my best to bite him when he came at me with that thing with the needle on the end of it.

But my gals told me to act nice, and since I'd taken the Pledge and sworn never to mess up again, I didn't bite him. But once.

And then he stuck me with that needle, and after that, I didn't much care what he did, because I fell into a big vat of warm molasses and just floated around.

Next thing I knew, we were back at the ranch. I opened my eyes and, much to my surprise, found myself in a cardboard box next to the woodstove—*in Sally May's living room*! I had two of the cutest little nurses a dog ever dreamed of having, and when they weren't stroking my head, they were bringing me bowls of warm milk.

Yes sir, right then and there I decided to go into the Hero business full-time. It would take a lot of that kind of treatment to wear me out.

Course, the one bad thing about it all was that I had to pack my leg around when I walked. They had that rascal bound up with tape and a metal splint, and I felt pretty peculiar trying to walk on it.

Around dark, Loper came home and the girls met him at the door and told him the whole story. He came over and knelt down beside my box and told me I was a "pretty good dog," which seemed a rather modest description but better than some of the things he had called me over the years. Or even that day.

Then Sally May hobbled in on her crutches and handed him the vet bill. His face turned red and his eyes almost bugged out of his head, and for a second there, I thought he was going to throw me out of the house. But he settled down.

"First you sprain my wife's ankle, then you get your own leg busted. In one day, you've become the only four hundred dollar dog I've ever owned." He held up the vet bill. "And look here, we even have papers on you now."

That got a big laugh. I missed the humor in it myself. I mean, if he was making snide remarks about my claim to being a prize-winning, top-of-the-line, blue-ribbon, papered, pedigreed cowdog . . . oh well. As long as they're laughing, they won't throw you out of the house. That's my motto.

Well, it was a wonderful holiday, one of my better Thanksgivings. Amy and Ashley camped out beside my box that night and took good care of me, and by noon of the next day, I was getting around on my peg leg.

I went into the kitchen, where Sally May was working on the Thanksgiving dinner. Not only did I build up a few points with the cook, but I also won a free turkey gizzard, which had a wonderful flavor but didn't chew any better than an old inner tube. I finally gave up trying to chew the thing and swallered it whole.

And did I mention the laughs we got when we walked through the house together? Yep, got some good laughs, Sally May hobbling along on her crutches and me coming along behind on my peg leg. That was the hit of the whole day.

Yes, it was a wonderful holiday. I mean, for once everything had turned out just right and couldn't have been bet. . . .

Oh, there was one little incident that cast a shadow. . . . I want to make it clear that it wasn't exactly my fault . . . yes, I had taken the Pledge and had sworn never to do anything wrong for the rest of my. . . .

You see, all the family had gone into the dining room and sat down to a big Thanksgiving feast and . . . well, they were all eating and I could hear their lips smacking . . . a guy naturally thinks of food when he hears six pairs of lips smacking and. . . .

How or why I wandered into the kitchen, I'm not sure. Maybe I was exercising. Yes, that was it, doing therapy, and wandered into the kitchen, so to speak, and found myself all alone. . . .

And there was this pie sitting on the counter—I mean, one lonely pie sitting there with no friends, nobody to talk to, no one with who or whom to share the holiday spirit, so naturally I . . .

I could smell it, see. PUNKIN PIE. Boy, do I like punkin pie! Well, I knew better than to . . . I mean, I'd taken the Pledge and everything and . . . I'd be the last guy in the world to. . . .

You won't believe this, but all of a sudden a gust of wind came through the winder, picked that whole pie up off the counter, and *knocked it on the floor.* Yes sir, just like that!

Well, you know me. When there's a mess to be cleaned up, I jump right in there and make a hand. I was in the process of trying to clean up the mess, and I mean cleaning it up in huge gulps, when. . . .

Oh well. I thought it was too stuffy in the house . . . a ranch dog has no business spending his time in a stuffy house and . . . I needed some fresh air, see, and. . . .

I spent the remainder of the holiday season outdoors, where I belonged.

When my girls left two days later, they hugged my neck and cried. And, fellers, when the girls are crying when they leave you, that's got to be a happy ending.